Danny MacNanny
and
the Rumbling Tum

Copyright © 2024 by Sue Wood-Skye
All rights reserved. This book or any portion thereof may not be reproduced or used in any manner whatsoever without the express written permission of the author except for the use of brief quotations in a book review.

Printed in the United Kingdom

First Edition 2024

Danny MacNanny
and
the Rumbling Tum
by
Sue Wood-Skye

Danny MacNanny was happy and bright,

In his fishing boat in the warm sunlight.

He cast out his line,

For the very first time.

He then waited for a fish to bite.

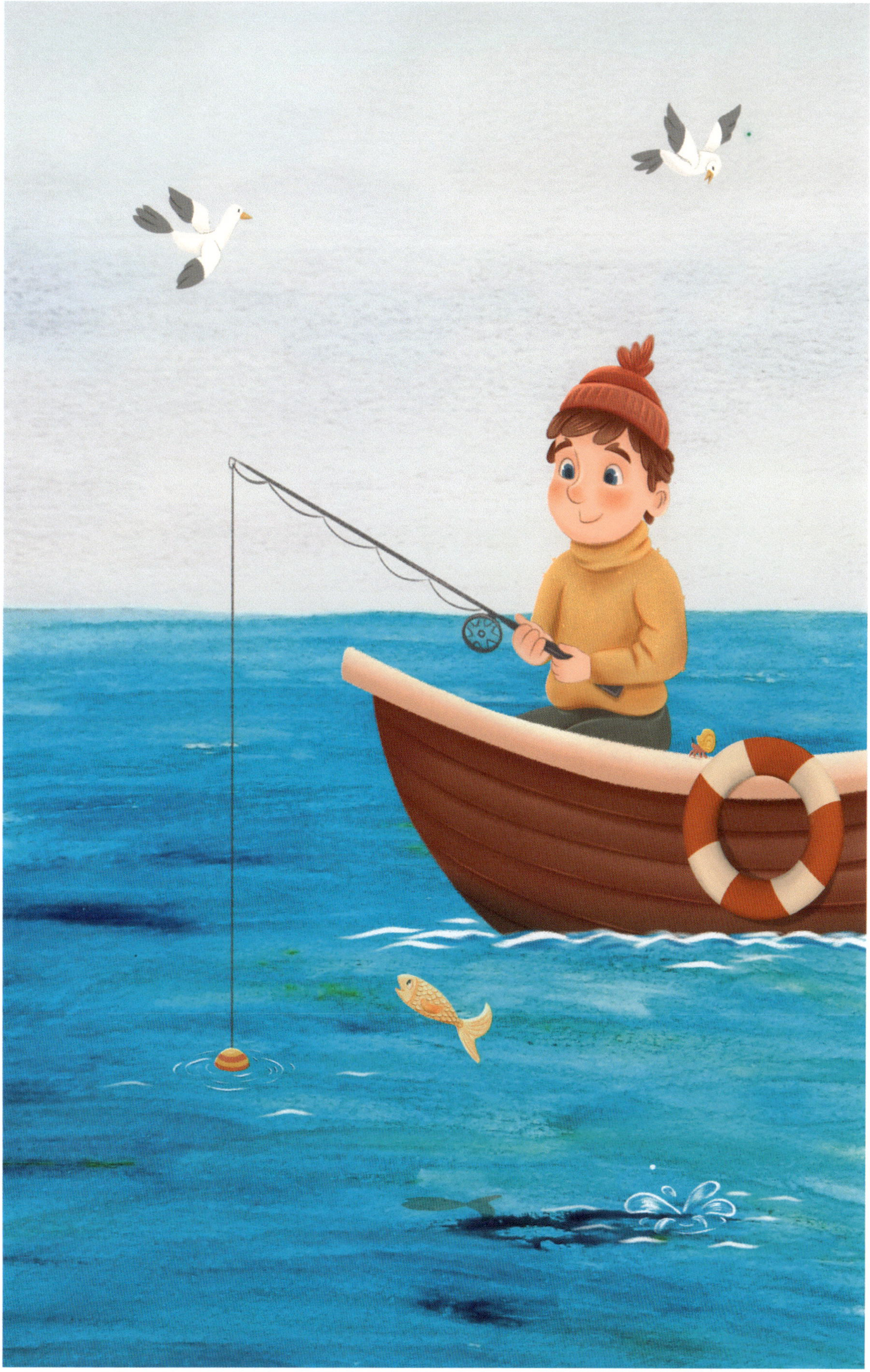

Tammy MacNanny sat on her stool,

Dreaming about some fishy stew.

"It's not much fun,

With a rumbling tum!"

She wished for a big fish too.

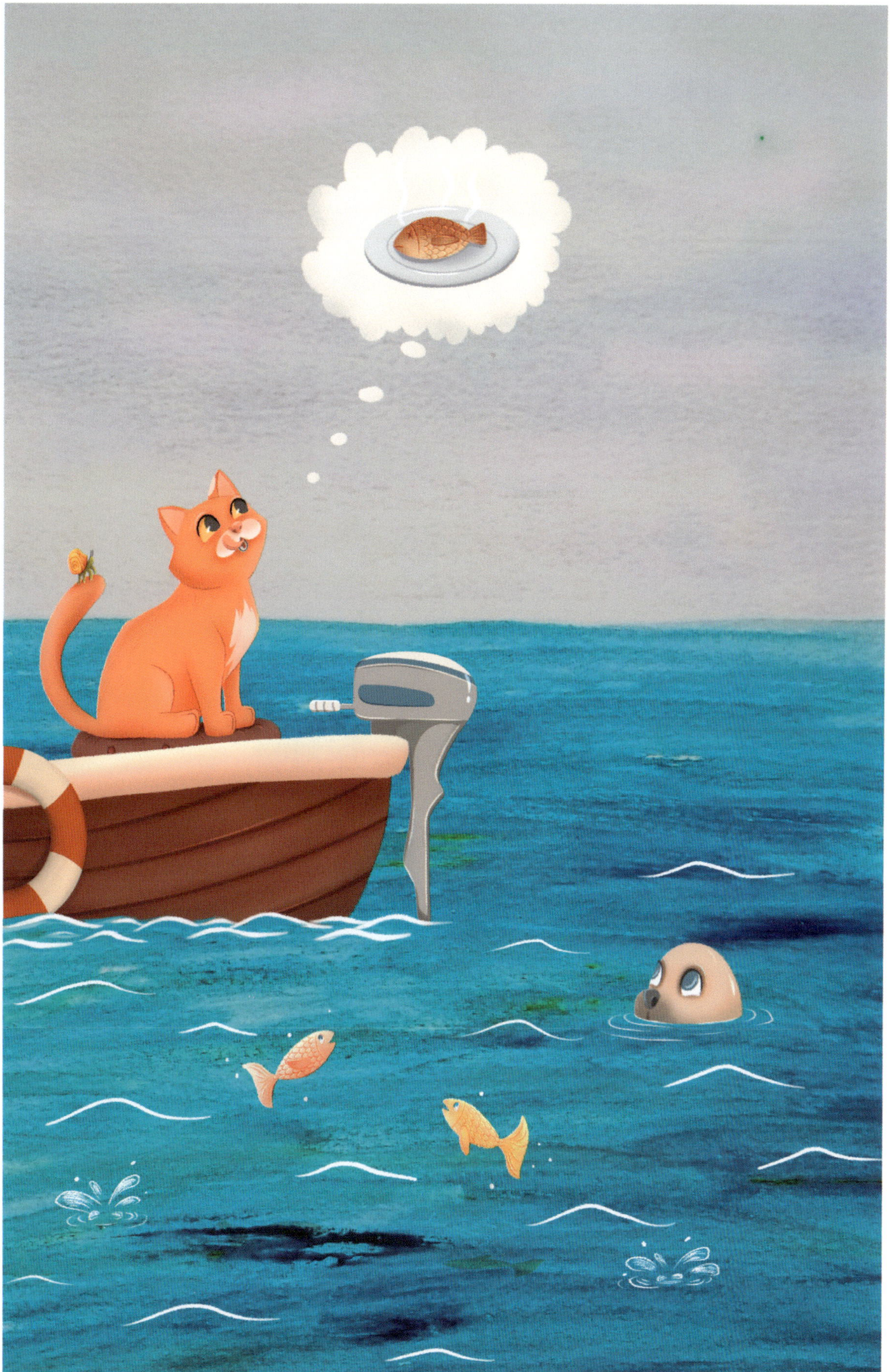

"I've caught a fish!"

Danny cried with glee.

"A great big fish for you and me."

On the end of the hook

Was a nail in a boot.

"I can't believe what I see!"

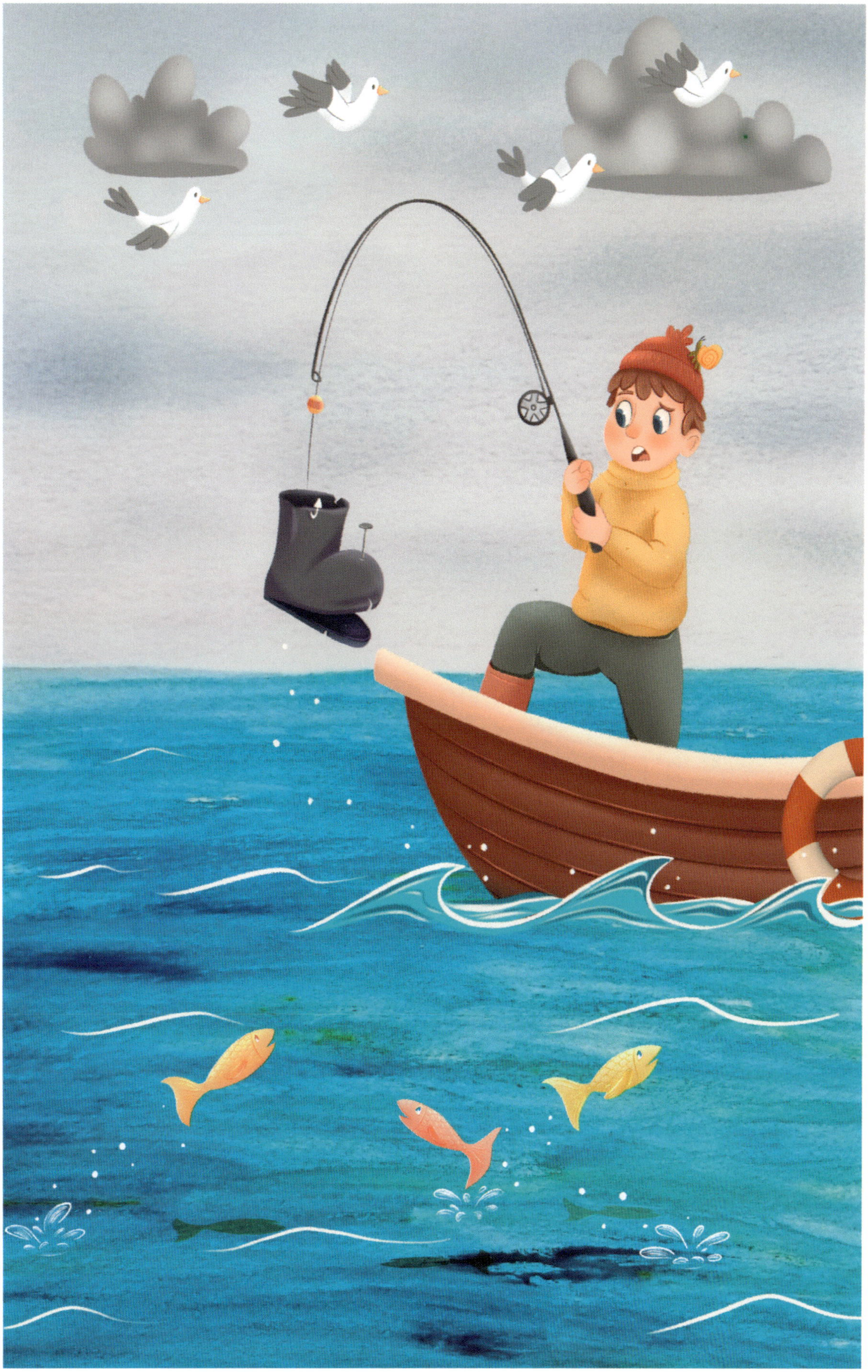

Tammy MacNanny, raised her eyes,

"A smelly old boot-Oh why, why, WHY!

It's not much fun,

With a rumbling tum.

If I don't eat soon, I will cry!"

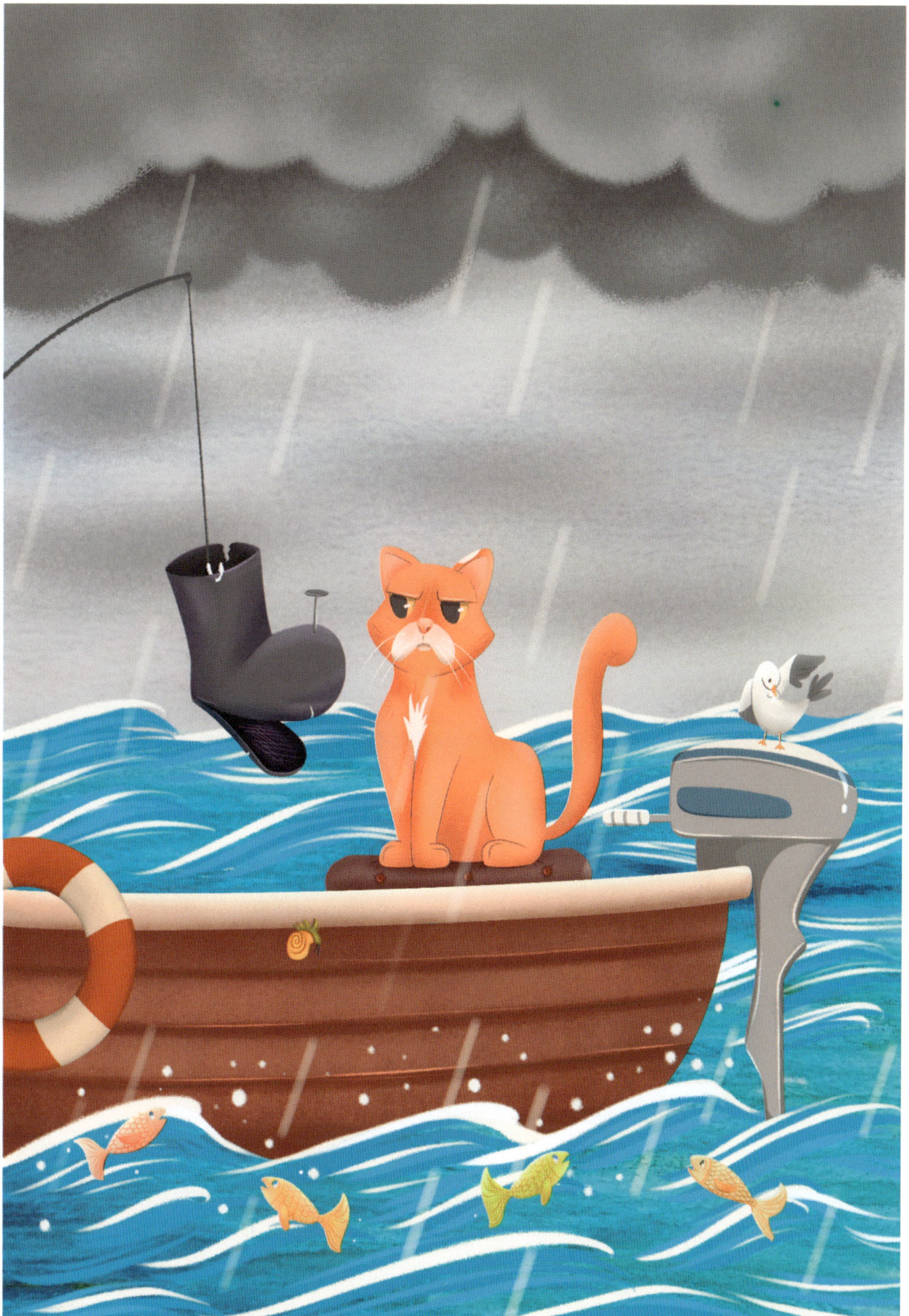

"I've caught a fish!" cried Danny so shrill,

"Pass the basket and start to fill."

On the end of the line,

Was a rusty road sign.

Danny began to feel rather ill.

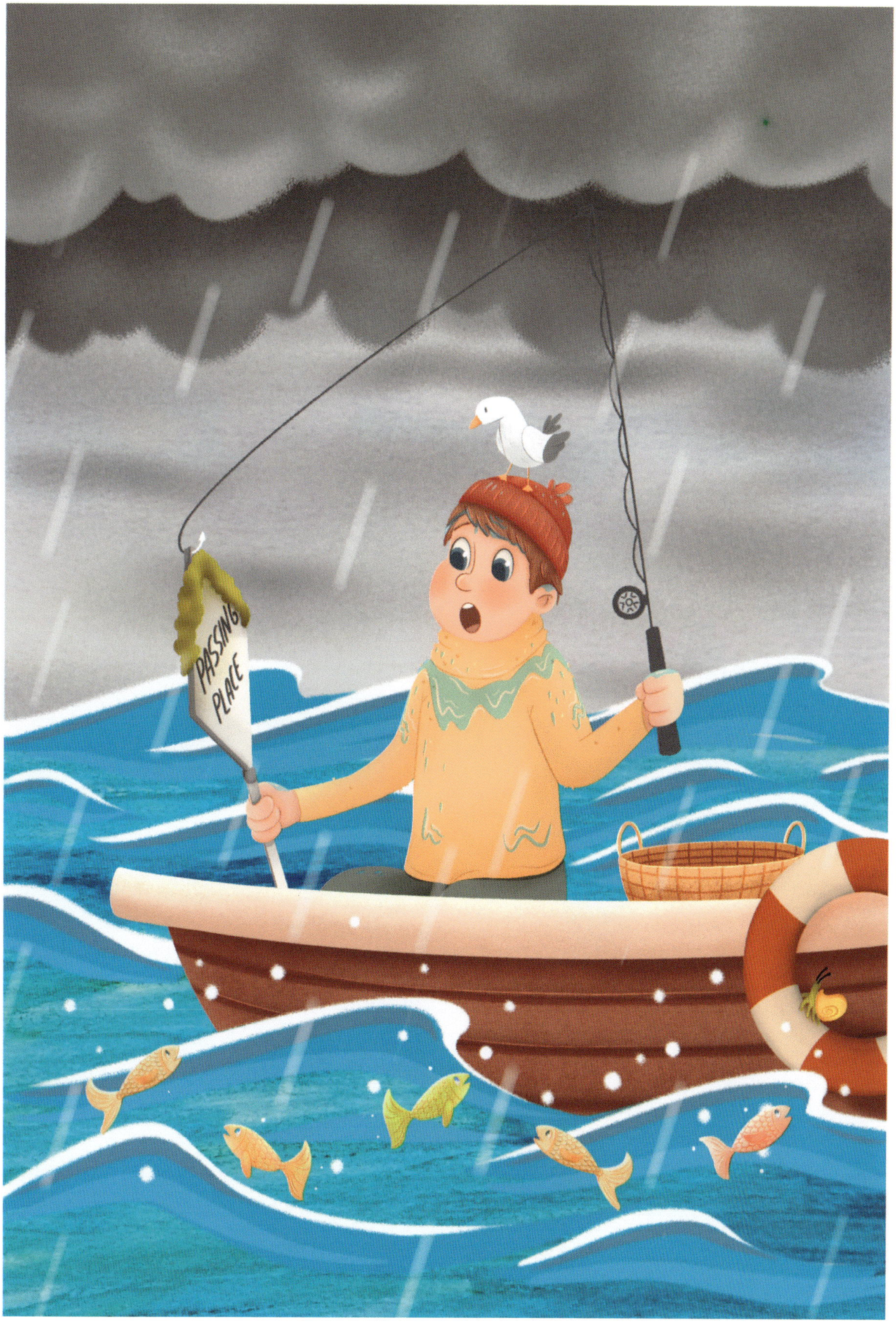
PASSING PLACE

Tammy MacNanny looked overboard:

"A rusty sign!" she loudly roared.

"It's not much fun,

With a rumbling tum"

Her grumpy mood-soared and soared.

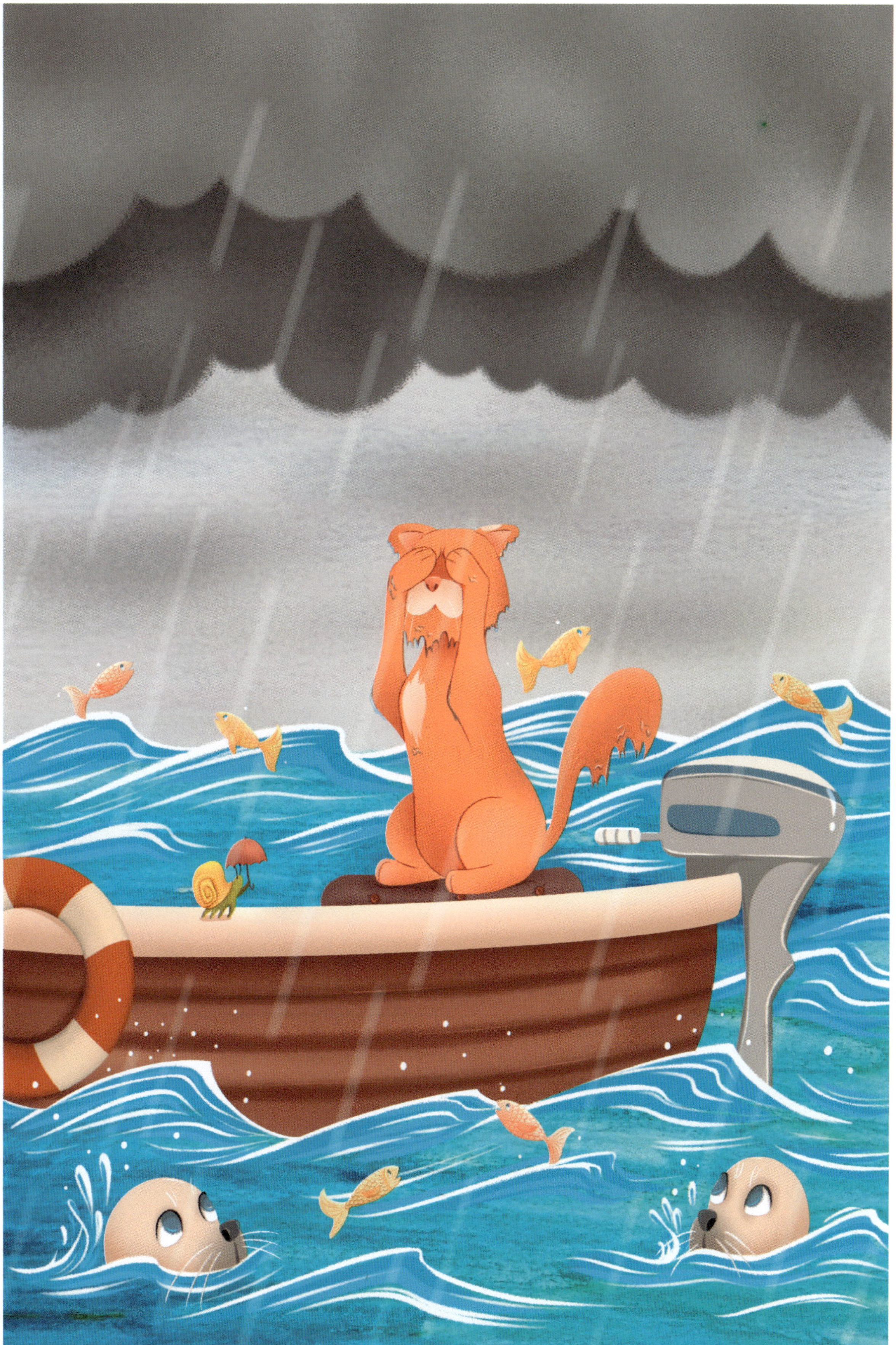

"I've caught a fish!" Danny yelled with a smile,

I told you just to wait a while."

Instead of a fish

Was a bright green dish.

"Oh…Goodness Tammy will be wild!"

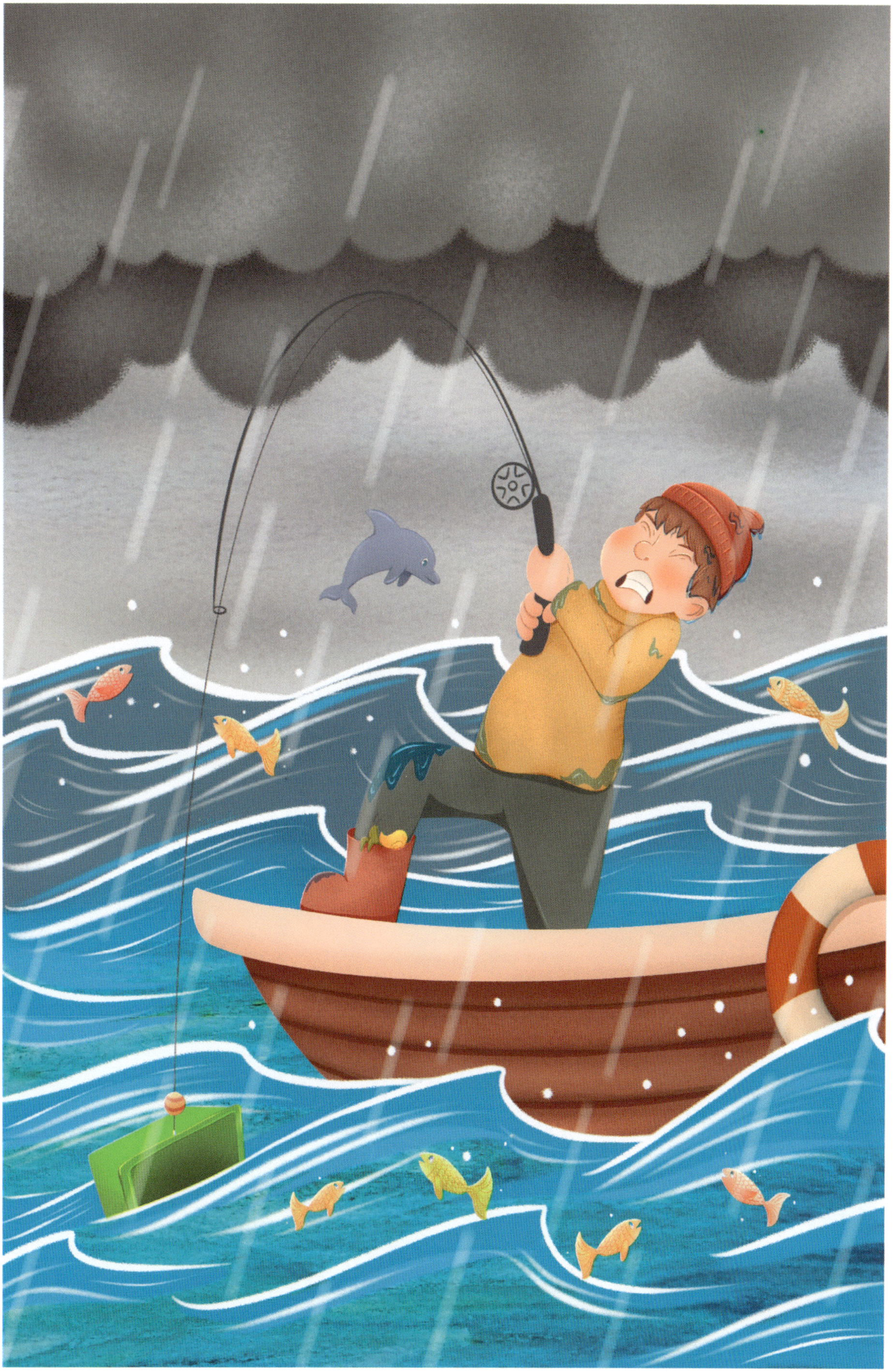

Tammy MacNanny pulled on her hat,

"No fish for me and That is That!

It's not much fun

With a rumbling tum.

I would be happy with a wee sprat."

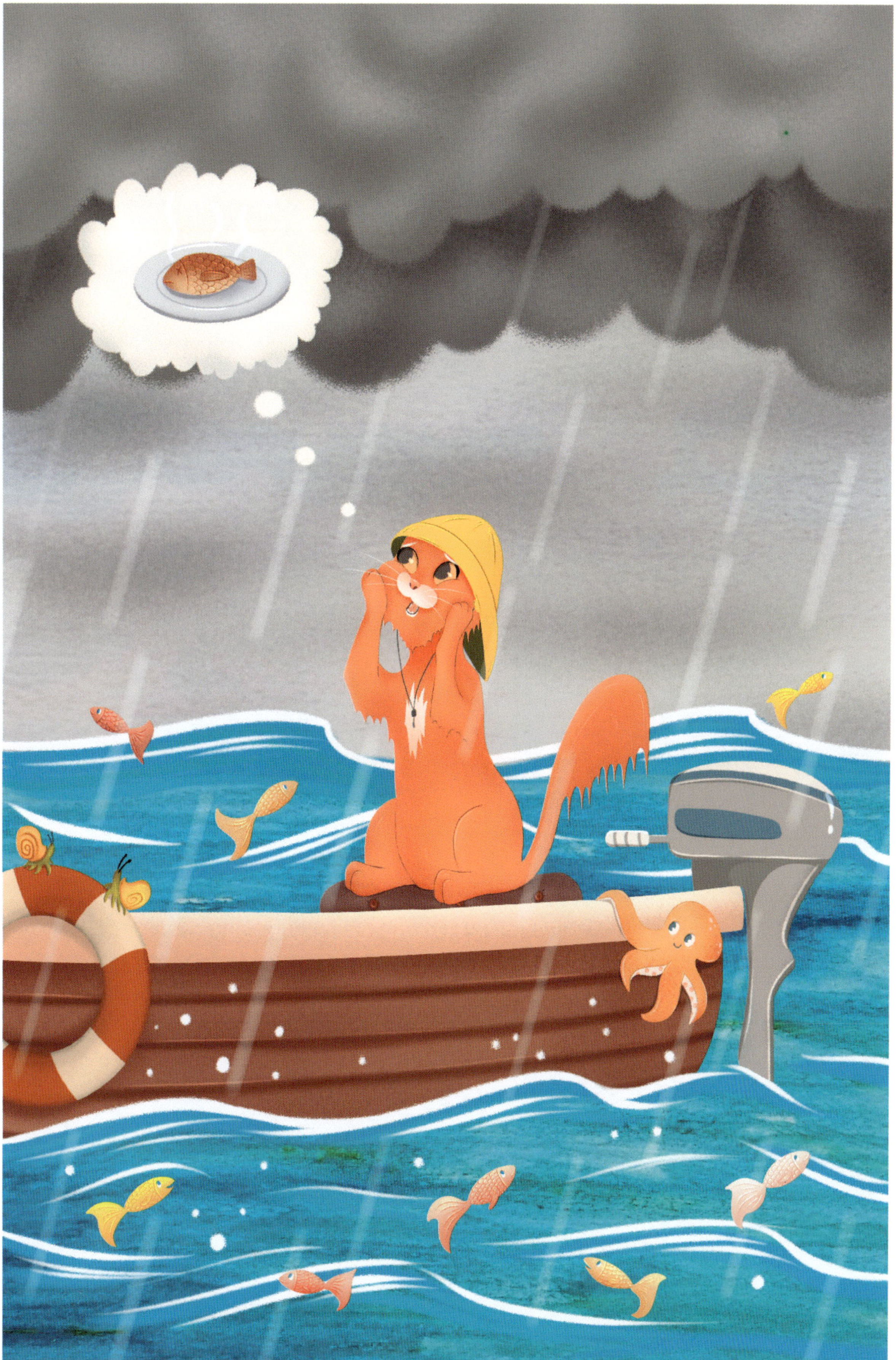

"I've caught a fish!" Danny cried with a squeal.

"Just wait and see, a perfect meal."

With a shake of his head,

He saw an old bed.

"Oh-No how will Tammy feel?"

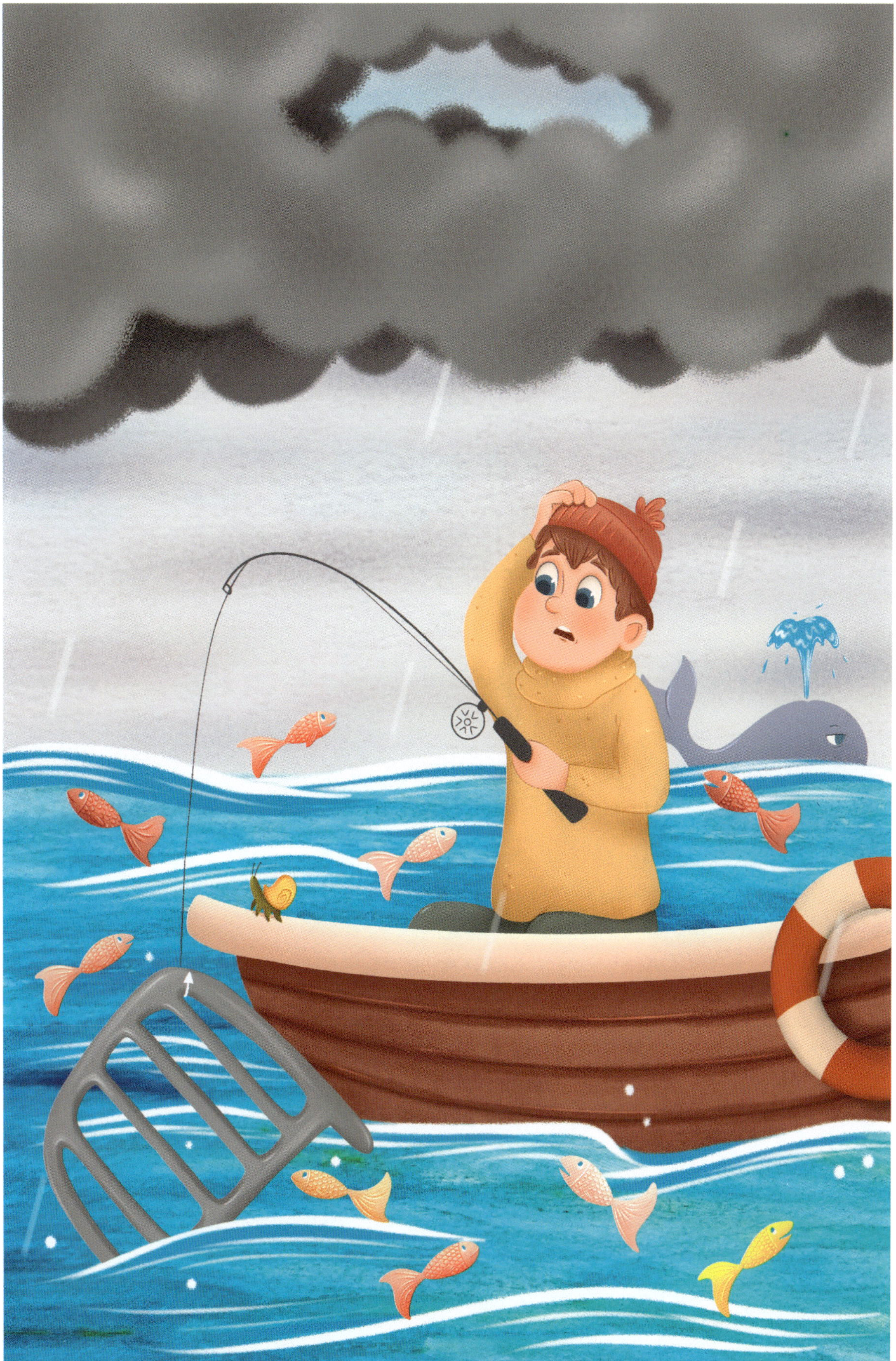

Tammy MacNanny rolled up her eyes,

She puffed her cheeks and blew out a sigh.

"It's not much fun,

With a rumbling tum."

She longed for a fish she, could try.

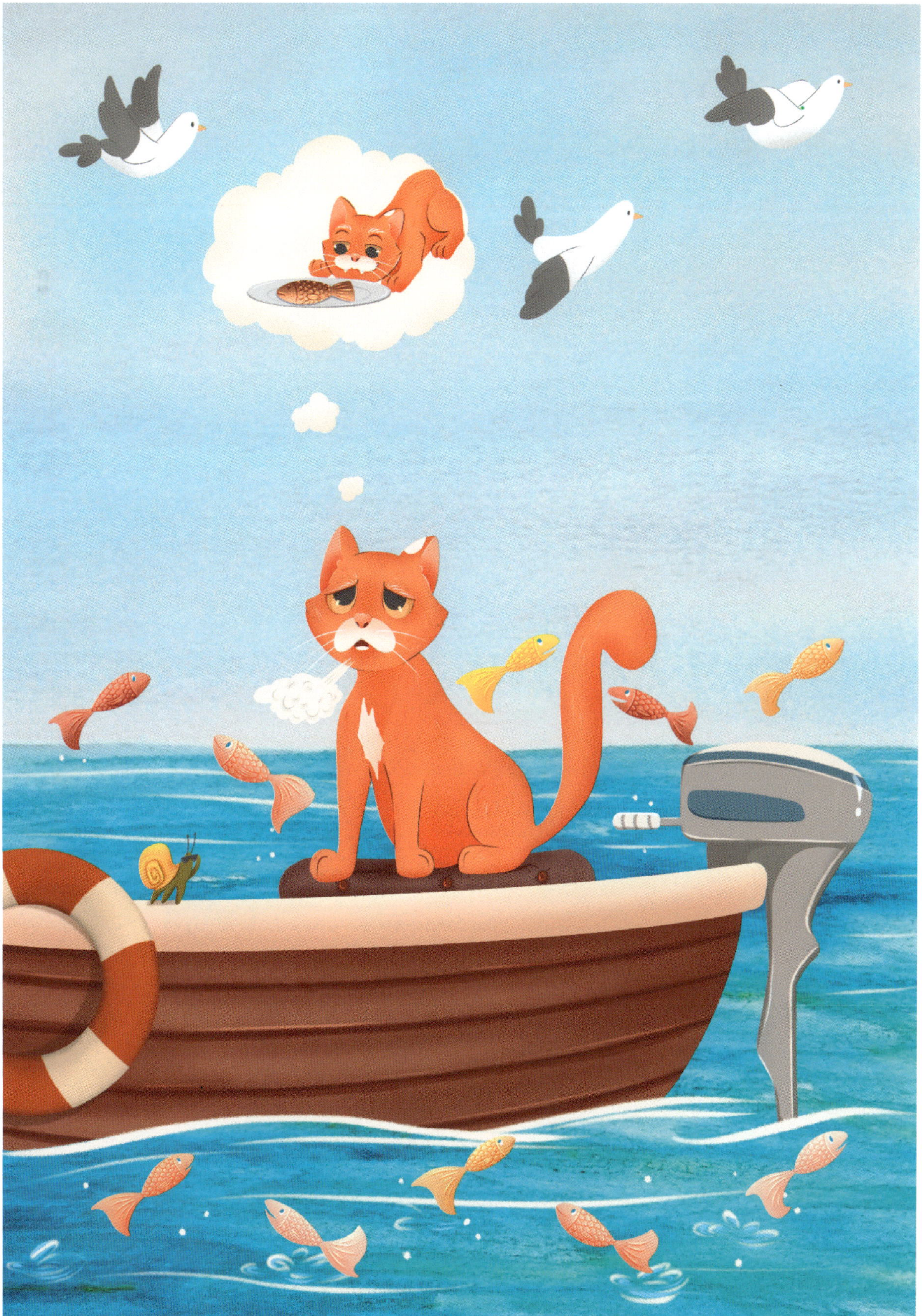

"I've caught a fish!" Danny cried with hope,

"It's big and fat; as big as a boat."

He moaned with a wail,

As he saw an old pail.

He hoped that Tammy would cope.

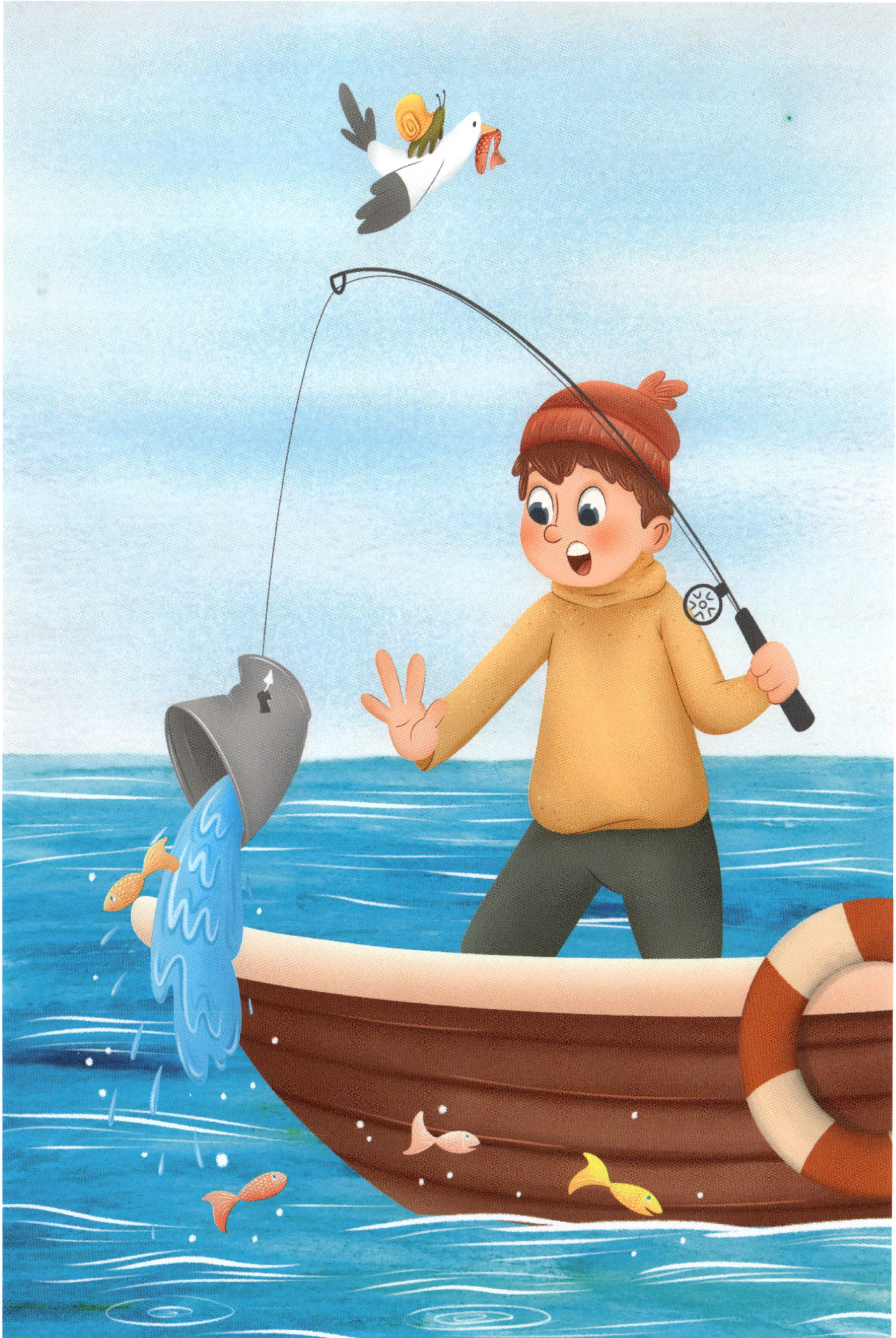

Danny winked and smiled with a sigh,

He laughed aloud with a glint in his eye.

"It's not much fun,

With a rumbling tum.

Let's hurry home for fish pie!"

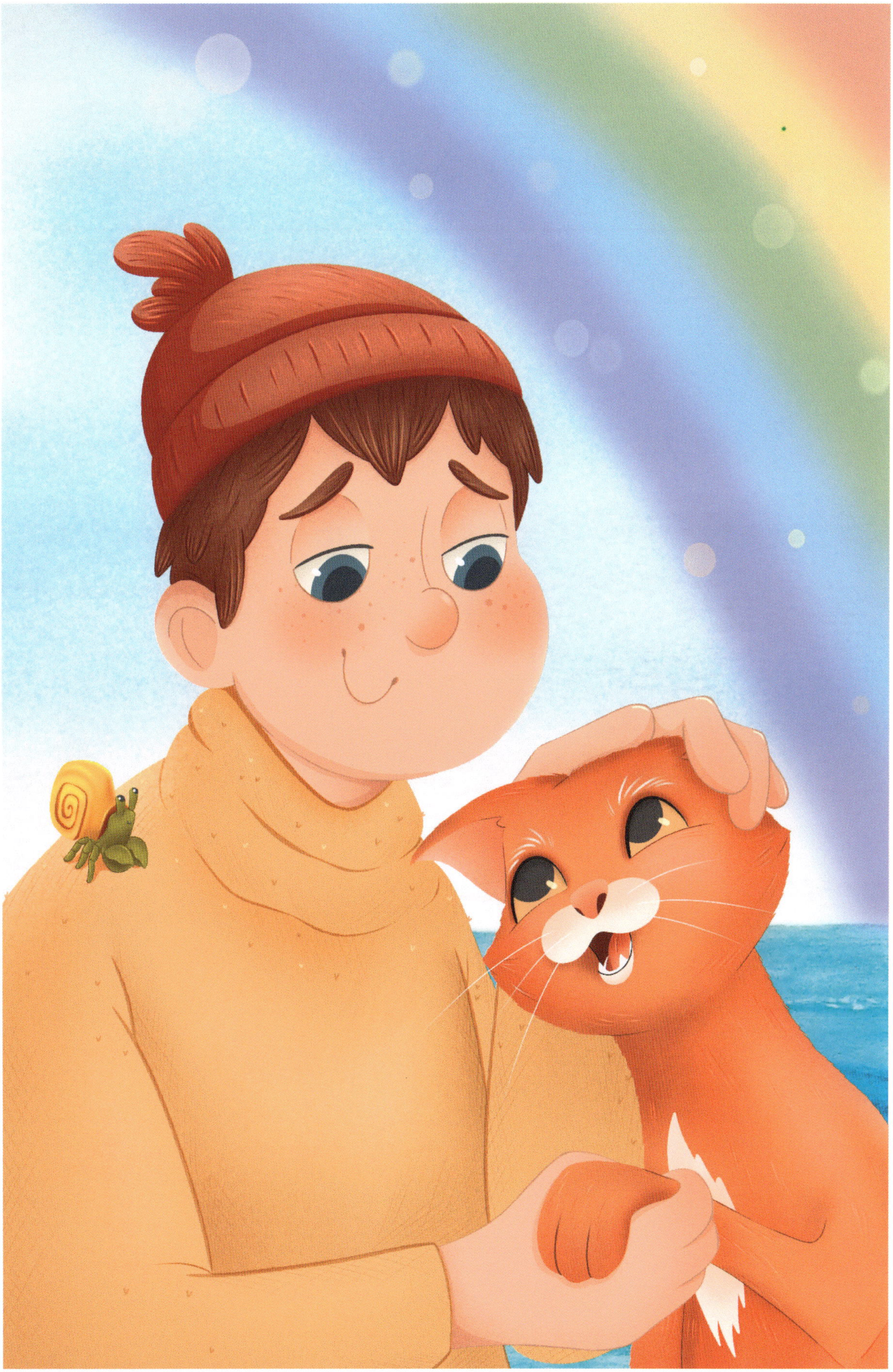

Later that day…

Danny and Tammy sat down with a smile,

On a garden bench, to rest a while.

"It's so much fun,

With a full-up tum!"

They looked at the junk in a pile.

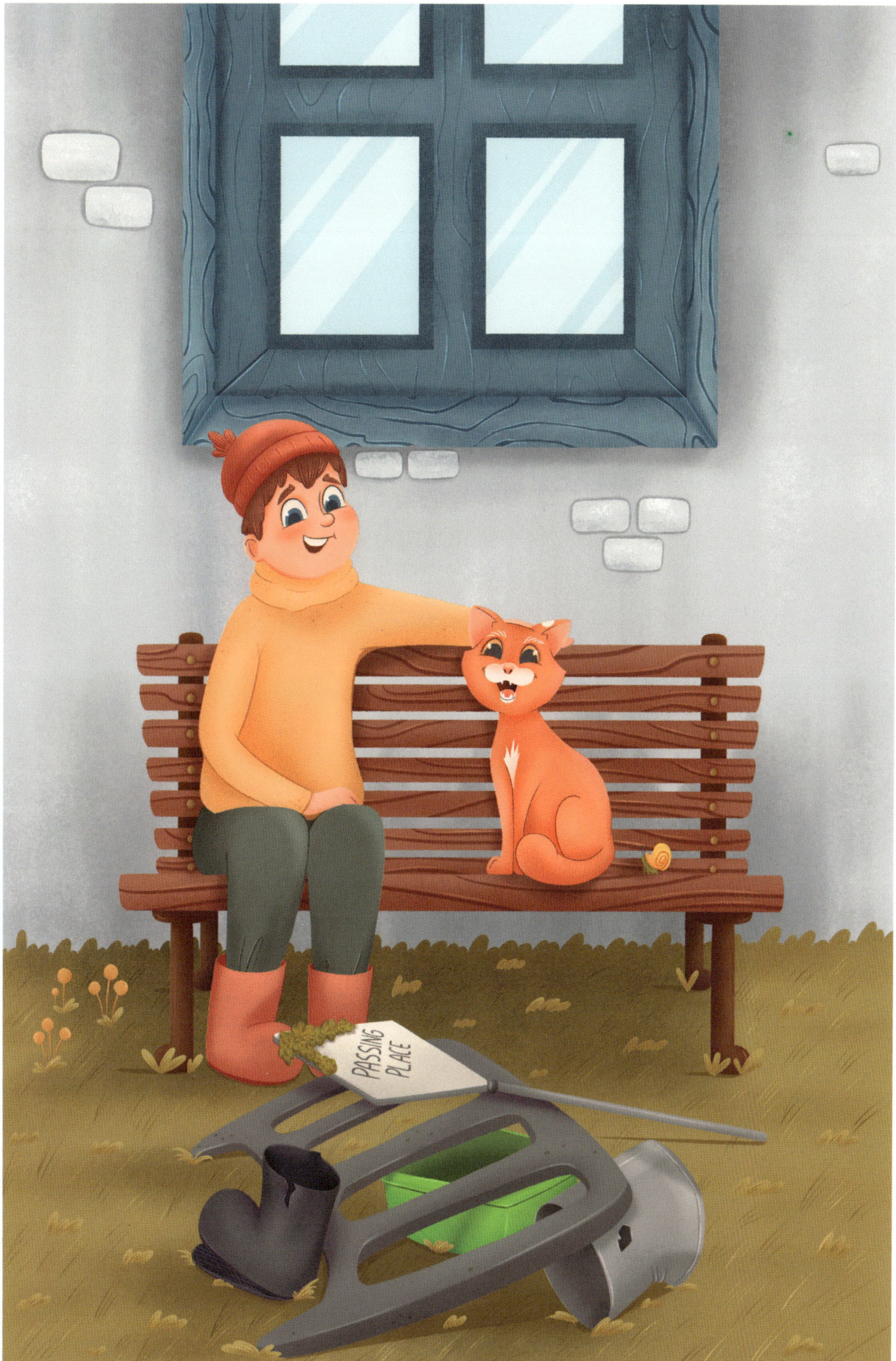
PASSING
PLACE

Danny and Tammy were busy in the sun,

Recycling junk was so much fun.

A bed, a boot with a nail,

A dish, a sign, and a pail.

"Yes-yes-yes…our work is done!"

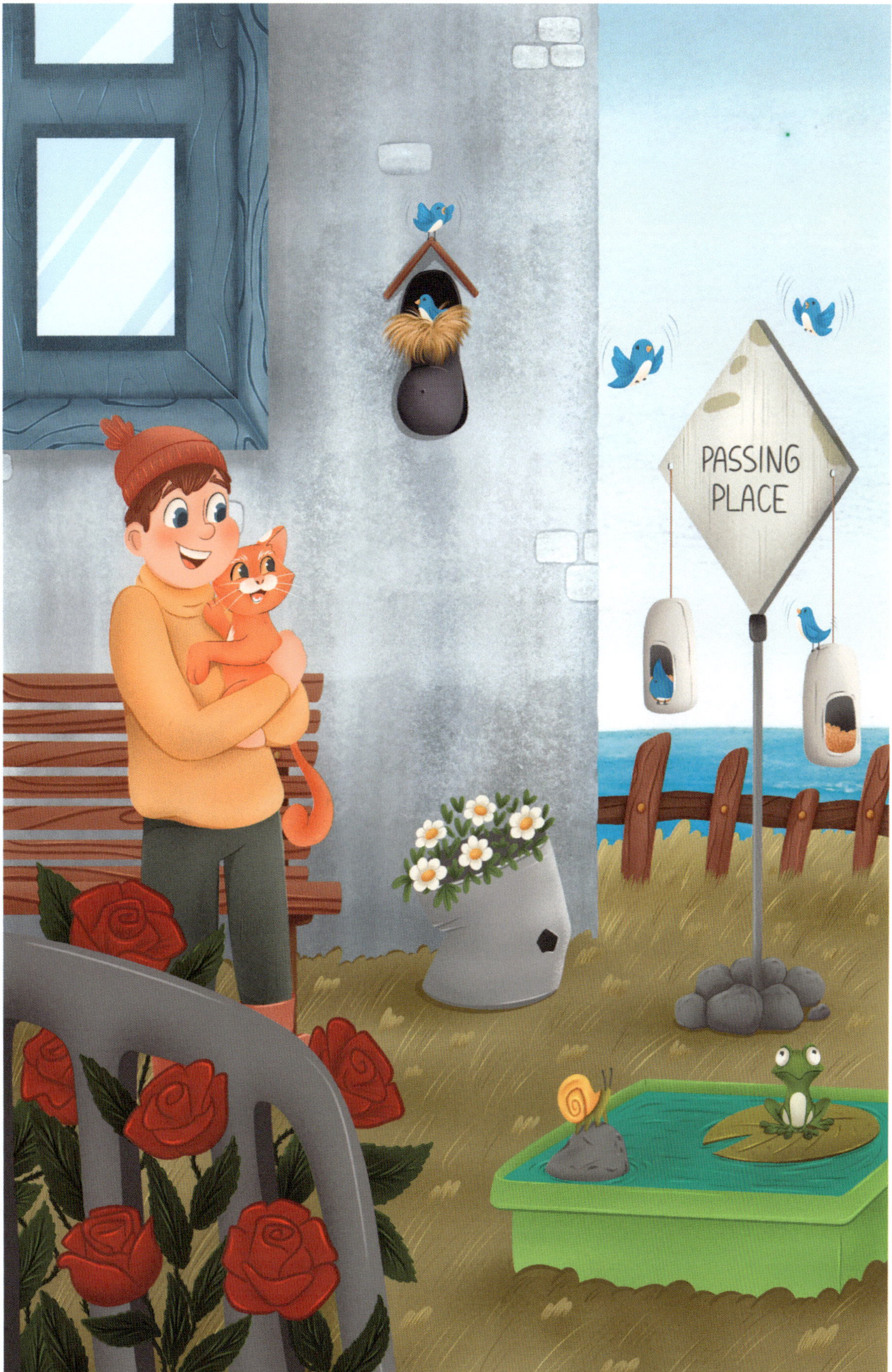
PASSING
PLACE

Save Our Sea Sides

Save our sea sides and keep them clean,

A day on the beach is a perfect dream.

Seaweed and seashells and barefoot in the sand,

Rock pools and tiny crabs tickling your hand.

Save our sea sides and keep them clean,

A day on the beach is a perfect dream.

Sue Wood-Skye

About the Author

Sue moved to the Isle of Skye almost 30 years ago from England. She immediately felt at home and found inspiration in the natural environment of Skye. Sue has published two poetry books and a haiku book, with Grosvenor House Publishing. Her poems have been published in several online journals and two literary magazines.

Sue's career spanning over 40 years was in the early years sector and finally a lecturer at the University of the Highlands and Islands. In 2021 Sue published her first children's book, **Muddy Moos and Midges** for a local children's mental wellbeing charity. After completing the book Sue realised this was where her passion lay- children's books. All of Sue's books have regularly reached the top fifty in their genre in Amazon's top 100.

Sue published her second children's book in 2023, **Here Come the Midges Run-Run-Run**, which was inspired by her free-range mischievous chickens running around her garden. In early 2024 Sue had three of her haiku poems and one painting featured in the **Prosetrics** magazine (January 2024 issue). This is where she met **Lana Grushnik** an illustrator living in Iceland. Sue contacted Lana to ask if she was interested in providing the illustrations for her new book **Danny MacNanny and the Rumbling Tum.** Lana was delighted to become involved and between them the story came to life. The first reading of the book will be in the grounds of Dunvegan castle in August 2024.

When Sue is not writing and painting, she enjoys rewilding her croft with native wildflowers, trees and shrubs. Sue and her husband Warren also run a successful hospitality business and meet guests from all over the world.

Printed in Great Britain
by Amazon